The Child's World®

Published in the United States of America by The Child's World®
1980 Lookout Drive • Mankato, MN 56003-1705
800-599-READ • www.childsworld.com

ACKNOWLEDGMENTS
The Child's World®: Mary Berendes, Publishing Director
The Design Lab: Kathleen Petelinsek, Design and Page Production
Literacy Consultants: Cecilia Minden, PhD, and Joanne Meier, PhD

LIBRARY OF CONGRESS
CATALOGING-IN-PUBLICATION DATA
Moncure, Jane Belk.
  My "i" sound box / by Jane Belk Moncure ;
illustrated by Rebecca Thornburgh.
    p. cm. — (Sound box books)
  Summary: "Little i has an adventure with items beginning with
her letter's sound, such as inchworms, iguanas, and an icy
igloo."—Provided by publisher.
  ISBN 978-1-60253-149-9 (library bound : alk. paper)
  [1. Alphabet.] I. Thornburgh, Rebecca McKillip, ill. II. Title. III.
Series.
  PZ7.M739Myi 2009
  [E]—dc22   2008033165

A NOTE TO PARENTS AND EDUCATORS:

Magic moon machines and five fat frogs are just a few of the fun things you can share with children by reading books with them. Reading aloud helps children in so many ways! It introduces them to new words, motivates them to develop their own reading skills, and expands their attention span and listening abilities. So it's important to find time each day to share a book or two . . . or three!

As you read with young children, you can help develop their understanding of how print works by talking about the parts of the book—the cover, the title, the illustrations, and the words that tell the story. As you read, use your finger to point to each word, modeling a gentle sweep from left to right.

Simple word games help develop important prereading skills, including an understanding of rhyme and alliteration (when words share the same beginning sound, such as "six" and "sand"). Try playing with words from a book you've just shared: "What other words start with the same sound as moon?" "Cat and hat, do those words rhyme?" The possibilities are endless—and so are the rewards!

My "i" Sound Box®

(This book concentrates on the short "i" sound in the story line. Words beginning with the long "i" sound are included at the end of the book.)

WRITTEN BY JANE BELK MONCURE

ILLUSTRATED BY REBECCA THORNBURGH

Little  had a box. "I will find things that begin with my **i** sound," she said. "I will put them into my sound box."

Little  went skip, skip, skip

up a hill.

She found inchworms, lots of
inchworms. The inchworms
wiggled and wiggled.

"What wiggly inchworms," she said.

Did she put the inchworms into

her box? She did.

Then Little  found iguanas,

lots of iguanas. The iguanas

wiggled and wiggled.

"What wiggly iguanas," she said.

She put the iguanas into the box

with the inchworms.

But the inchworms did not like
the iguanas!

The inchworms jumped out of

the box.

The iguanas jumped out, too.

Away they went!

Little  could not find the inchworms or the iguanas.

They were hiding.

Then Little  found an igloo.

Did she put the igloo into her

 box? She did.

Just then, the sun came out. Can
you guess what happened?

The igloo melted!

"Now who will help me fill my

box?" she said.

A friend came by.

"I will help you," he said. "We  can fill your box with insects."

First they found big green insects.

Lots of big green insects.

Next they found yellow insects

and brown insects.

Then they found red-and-black insects.

"What else can we do?" said

Little .

"We can make an insect zoo."

You can visit it, too.

Little 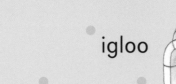's Word List

igloo

iguana

inchworm

insect

Other Words with the Short "i" Sound

inch

ink

instruments

infant

inn

invitation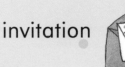

Words with the Long "i" Sound

Little "i" has another sound in some words. She says her name, "i."
Can you read these words? Listen for Little "i's" name.

ice

ice skates

island

ice cream

iron

ivy

More to Do!

In this book, Little [image] and her friend made an insect zoo. You can imagine that you are helping them collect even more insects. Count the insects as they come inside. Use dried beans or chips to help you find the answers.

Help Little [image] count:

1. Some red insects came first. There were 3 little insects. Next came 4 brown insects. How many red and brown insects are in the insect zoo?

2. Some yellow insects came next. There were 6. Next came 2 black insects. How many yellow and black insects are in the insect zoo?